Lost in Boggley

This story shows the value of makin

Story by:
Will Ryan

Treatment by:
Lenny Levitt

Illustrated by:

David High
Russell Hicks
Douglas McCarthy
Allyn Conley-Gorniak
Julie Ann Armstrong

Lorann Downer
Rivka
Matthew Bates
Fay Whitemountain
Marilyn Gage

WORLDS OF WONDER™

Worlds of Wonder, Inc. is the exclusive licensee, manufacturer and distributor of The World of Teddy Ruxpin toys.
"The World of Teddy Ruxpin" and "Teddy Ruxpin" are trademarks of Alchemy II, Inc., Chatsworth, CA.
The symbol **W•W** and "Worlds of Wonder" are trademarks of Worlds of Wonder, Inc., Fremont, California.

Grubby™ Newton Gimmick™ Princess Aruzia™ Leota™ Wooly What's-It™ Fobs®

Prince Arin™

Teddy

Hello. I'm Teddy Ruxpin, and I'd like to tell you a story.

Grubby

Am I in the story?

Teddy

Why yes, you are, Grubby.

Grubby

Oh, boy! This sounds like a good story.. so far.

Teddy

Well, one day Gimmick, Grubby and I went on a hike into a part of Boggley Woods none of us had ever visited before.

Page 1

Grubby

Wow! Look at all the bright leaves on these trees!

Teddy

This must be the most beautiful part of the entire forest, Gimmick!

Gimmick

You're right, Teddy...and it's just perfect for that little surprise I told you about. We're going to spend the whole morning painting these lovely trees!

Teddy

Painting? Oh, boy! Let's get started!

Grubby

Gee, these trees don't look like they need paintin'. They're already colorful!

Teddy

No, Grubby...we're not going to paint the trees...we're going to paint pictures of the trees.

Grubby

Oh!

Teddy

So, we got out our brushes and paper, and Gimmick and I started painting. But Grubby just stood there looking a little confused.

Grubby

Gee.

Teddy

What's wrong, Grubby? Don't you want to paint these beautiful trees?

Grubby

Yeah, I'd like to, but it's so confusin'!

Gimmick

What's confusing, Grubby?

Grubby

All those colors. There must be millions of 'em.

Teddy

Colors aren't that confusing, Grubby! There are really only three.

Grubby

Three? What do ya mean?

"Red and Yellow and Blue"

Nearly every color you see
Can be mixed together from only three.
Now, the first is red, yellow's number two
And the final color is known as blue.

There's a lot that you can do
With red and yellow and blue.
You can make new colors for days and days
When you mix 'em up in different ways.
There's a rainbow there for you
In red and yellow and blue.

To make orange you mix yellow
With an equal amount of red,
But if you want some purple
Mix blue with the red instead.

Do you mean to say these are all I need
To mix any color I see?
Just about, but it might be right
To add black and white for dark and light!

There's a lot that you can do
With red and yellow and blue.
You can make new colors for days and da
When you mix 'em up in different ways.
There's a rainbow there for you
In red and yellow and blue.

Now mix one part yellow
With one part blue
And gradually you will get green.
Now add some white and a little more blu
Hey, looky, aquamarine!

There's a lot that you can do
With red and yellow and blue.
You can make new colors for days and da
When you mix 'em up in different ways.
There's a rainbow there for you
In red and yellow,
Not brown and burgundy,
Red and yellow and blue.
Red and yellow and blue.

Teddy

Soon Grubby started painting pictures of the trees, too.

Grubby

Yeah, and with lots of colors!

Teddy

After a while, we all decided to go off in different directions so we could paint as many different trees as possible.

Grubby

Yep, and we agreed to meet later on by the big funny lookin' tree with bright blue leaves.

Gimmick

Okay! Meet you back here by the big blue tree!

Teddy

But a little while later, when Gimmick went back to find the big blue tree, it wasn't there!

Gimmick

How odd. There's a funny looking tree with bright yellow leaves, but no funny looking tree with bright blue leaves.

Well, I'll just have to keep looking, I guess.

Teddy

Things were getting very strange! Gimmick thought he heard giggling sounds coming from the tree!

Gimmick

Sometimes I imagine the silliest things!

Teddy

And the same thing happened to Grubby.

Grubby

When I tried to find my way back to the big blue tree, I could only find a funny lookin' tree with bright red leaves. Not only was I lost, but I kept hearin' little gigglin' sounds, too.

Teddy

And when I went back to find the big blue tree, I could only find a funny looking tree with leaves that were purple.

Grubby

...which is a combination of red and blue.

Teddy

Blue tree, purple tree...I was so confused!

Where's the funny looking blue tree...and where are Gimmick and Grubby?

Which way do I go now?

Voices

I don't know which way to go!
Don't ask me! Hee hee hee!
Which way, which way,
which way ya say?

Teddy

Hey, who said that?

Voices

Not me. Not I. Me either.
Maybe it was him. Maybe it was neither!

Teddy

The mysterious voices seemed to be coming from the funny looking tree that I had thought was purple...but now it was orange!

Hey, is anybody in that tree?

Voices

No!!

Grubby

Hey! What's all the shoutin' about? Oh, hi, Teddy! Boy, am I glad I found you!

Gimmick

Teddy! Grubby! I thought I heard some voices!

Grubby

Yeah, who were ya talkin' to, Teddy?

Teddy

Well...

Voices

Not to us. Uh-uh, not us. Somebody else. Maybe Gus!

Teddy

Wow! A talking tree!

Gimmick

That's no talking tree, Teddy.

Teddy

Then what's going on, Gimmick?

Gimmick

Heavens to Grundo! I believe we've discovered the legendary Boggleberry Tree. I understand it's the home of the Wogglies!

Grubby
The Wogglies?!

Teddy
How's that?

Teddy
Well, what are the Wogglies?

Gimmick
Well, I'm not sure. I've never actually seen one, but if there are really any Wogglies hiding in those branches, there's one way to find out.

Gimmick
According to an old story I once read, this should do the trick. Repeat loudly after me.."Ogglie Ogglie Woggley, come out, come out, come out!"

Teddy & Grubby
Ogglie Ogglie Woggley, come out, come out, come out!

Teddy

Suddenly, out of the tree hopped the cutest little creatures we had ever seen!

Gimmick

Oh, look! There they are!

Grubby

They were just about Fob-sized.

Teddy

And they were laughing and hopping all around us!

Gramps

Well, how do ya do? How do ya do? I'm Gramps Woggley. Who are you?

Teddy

Why hello, Gramps. I'm Teddy Ruxpin, and these are my friends, Grubby and Newton Gimmick.

Wogglies

Hello. Hello. How do ya do? Pleased to meet ya. How are you?

Teddy

Well, if you Wogglies live here, Gramps,
then this must be the Boggleberry Tree.

Gramps

That it is. Oh, yes siree!
For generations we've lived in this tree.

Wogglies

Yes, we have! Yes, we do!
It's true! It's true! It's true! It's true!

Gimmick

Then that explains why none of us
could find the funny looking tree
with the bright blue leaves.

Teddy

Why's that, Gimmick?

Gimmick

Because this is the funny looking tree with the bright blue leaves, but it isn't blue right now…it's orange.

Grubby

Hey, look! The leaves are changin' color again!

Teddy

And, sure enough, the funny looking tree with bright orange leaves turned back into a funny looking tree with bright blue leaves…right before our very eyes!

Grubby

Wow!

Gimmick

Heavens to Grundo!

Teddy

That's amazing!

Gramps

That's not really as amazing as it may first appear.
Ya see, it happens all the time around here.

Gimmick

A tree that changes colors all the time.

Teddy

Oh, I see. So we were at the right tree all along.

Gimmick

Yes, precisely!

Teddy

It seems as though you Wogglies really enjoy living here in Boggley Woods!

Gramps

Oh, yes we do. This is very true.
It's a beautiful part of the forest, too!
But we meet so few travelers passin' through.

Grubby

Guess they don't wanna get lost.

Wiggs

But that gives us lots and lots of space for leaping and jumping all over the place!

Gramps

This is Wiggs, yep, Wiggs is his name. He's our best jumper!

Wiggs

Yeah, that's my game!

Grubby

No wonder, look at those feet!

Teddy

The Wogglies spoke in rhyme, almost all the time! And they were having so much fun jumping and swinging from the branches of the Boggleberry Tree that we decided to join them.

Grubby

Then they started singin', which is kinda like the way they talk, only with music, and we joined 'em in that, too!

"The Wogglies of the Boggley Woods"

We're the Wogglies,
The Wogglies,
The Wogglies of the Boggley Woods.
You'll probably boggle
And giggle and goggle—
A logical likelihood—
'Cause they're the Wogglies,
The Wogglies,
The Wogglies of the Boggley Woods.

When they feel ecstatic,
They're very acrobatic,
And hardly ever static! It's true!
It's true!
They're elastically gymnastic.
Performin' feats fantastic,
Very enthusiastically, too!

'Cause they're the Wogglies,
The Wogglies,
The Wogglies of the Boggley Woods.
You'll probably boggle
And giggle and goggle—
A logical likelihood—
To see the Wogglies,
The Wogglies,
The Wogglies of the Boggley Woods.

They reside in the vicinity
Of the Boggleberry Tree
In case you're wonderin' where they can
  be found.
It's true! It's true!
And though leaping is their favorite thing
They also love to laugh and sing.
And they're really fond of jumpin' up
  and down.
Up and down.

'Cause they're the Wogglies,
The Wogglies,
The Wogglies of the Boggley Woods.
You'll probably boggle
And giggle and goggle—
A logical likelihood—
To see the Wogglies,
The Wogglies,
The Wogglies of the Boggley Woods.

Laughin' and thumpin',
And singin' and jumpin',
And doin' what Wogglies should.
'Cause we're the Wogglies.
Wogglies,
Wogglies,
Wogglies
Of Boggley Woods.

Teddy

You Wogglies have as much fun singing as Fobs do!

Gramps

That shouldn't be a big surprise.
We're relatives, ya realize.

Grubby

Oh yeah, I thought you guys looked kinda familiar.

Gramps

Ah, but there's many a difference, yes siree,
between a Fob and a Woggley.

Teddy

Oh?

Wiggs

Our feet are bigger, I'm proud to say.
That helps us jump around all day!

Grubby

Wow! I'll say!

Gramps

And our ears, you'll note, are nice
and large.
That's how we Wogglies hear
the sounds of trolls and Bounders
and whatever may come near.

Teddy

I see.

Wiggs

We've lots of friends here in the woods.
So, whenever we hear a stranger,
we use our feet to jump and thump
and warn ourselves of danger.

Teddy

That makes sense.

Gimmick

Precisely.

Gramps

There are many Wogglies, as you can see,
and all of us live in our Family Tree.

Grubby

Brothers 'n sisters 'n uncles 'n cousins?

Gramps

Yep! We Wogglies live here by the dozens!

Teddy

So different branches of the Woggley
family live on different branches of the
Boggleberry Tree?

Wiggs

That's right!
It's nice to watch the colors change,
and it makes us all feel merry
to be so near our favorite food…

Wogglies

…fresh Boggleberries!

Grubby

They must be loaded with bounce!

Teddy

After a while, it was time to go home, but we wanted to thank the Wogglies for all the fun we had with them.

Gramps, we would like you to have our paintings of the trees of Boggley Woods.

Gimmick

Good idea, Teddy!

Grubby

Yeah, ya might enjoy lookin' at some trees that don't change color all the time.

Gramps

On behalf of all Wogglies, I'm happy to say "thanks" for these paintings you've given us today.

Wogglies

Yes! Thank you. How nice. Hooray! Hooray!

Teddy

Oh, that's alright. It's been a delight.

Wiggs

And now it's time, I think we should guide you out of this part of the woods.

Teddy

Why, thank you!

Grubby

I wondered how we were gonna get outa' here.

Gramps

It's the very least that we could do to really give our thanks to you.

Teddy

Gee, I wish we could've made a painting of your Boggleberry Tree.

Gimmick

But, Teddy, an accurate painting of a tree whose leaves change color constantly is scientifically impossible!

Teddy

As the Wogglies helped us find our way back, they explained to Gimmick how it was scientifically possible to make an accurate painting of a Boggleberry Tree.

Gramps

You can do it, it's my belief,
if ya use the Boggleberry leaf.

Grubby

Huh? Paint with a buncha leaves?

Gramps

Grind up the leaves to form a paint,
that's kind of magic, strange and quaint
What's painted with it, you will see,
changes colors constantly!

Gimmick

That's brilliant! Now why didn't I think of that?

Grubby

When we got home, Gimmick tried it, and it really worked!

Teddy

Gimmick named this discovery after our new friends and the tree they live in! So, if we hadn't been lost in Boggley Woods and met the Wogglies, we'd never've known about the newest color in the world!

Grubby

You're right, Teddy. It's a color that keeps on changin', called...

All

...WOGGLEBOGGLE!

Grubby

And just think, Woggleboggle contains red and yellow and blue.

Gimmick

Yes...precisely.

There's a lot that you can do
With red and yellow and blue.
You can make new colors for days and days
When you mix 'em up in different ways.
There's a rainbow there for you
In red and yellow,
Not brown and burgundy,
Red and yellow and blue.
Red and yellow and blue.